LIFEGUARD ON DUTY

ZESTY CORN CHIPS

Don't waste your time
looking at the boring
copyright stuff.

For Dad

About This Book

The illustrations for this book were created using scanned mixed media and Kyle T. Webster brushes in Photoshop. This book was edited by Deirdre Jones and designed by Saho Fujii and Jamie W. Yee. The production was supervised by Erika Schwartz, and the production editor was Jen Graham. The text was set in Smug Seagull, and the display type is hand-lettered.

SMUG SEAGULL

If you want to see
something exciting,
watch this....

maddie frost

LB

Little, Brown and Company
New York Boston

Get a good look, because I just so happen to be the best snack swiper from shore to shore.

That's a fact!

Being the best means I got guts. I strike while the sun is hot, if you know what I'm saying.

SWIPE

Are you keeping up? Because I'm just getting started!

Walk with me, talk with me.
Being the best is a big deal.

I got my name in lights!

I got my name in the sky.

People come from miles away to capture my beauty.

The fans go crazy when I'm around!

ARF! ARF! ARF! ARF! ARF! ARF!

I even have my own signature dance move.

With one of these!

And these!

Slide to the right.

All in the core.

Say, Short Stuff, that's one scrumptious-looking french fry you got there.

Mind if I have a—

Give me a—

Let me take a—

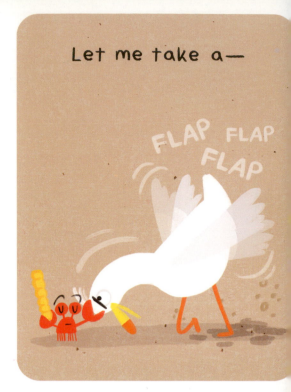

Hey, look! A rainbow!

Like I always say, you gotta be tough.

You gotta be—

POP

PFFFFFFFF

SWIPE

All right, listen up, Short Stuff. Nobody, I mean NOBODY, swipes from me!

Don't you know who I am?

Didn't you read my sign?

Well, pal, I just so happen to be the—

PLIP

SAND!
I love you, sand!

MWAH
MWAH
MWAH

Ahem —I mean...
I got a cramp
in my wing, see?

And I stubbed
my toe, see?

So I'll just swipe myself another snack.
Yeah! Because I can swipe anything I
feel like. No doubt about it.

I...I....I...

I've lost my swipe.

This is the end. Goodbye, signs!

Goodbye, fans!

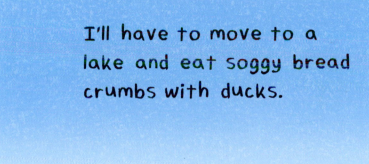

Goodbye, special lookout tower handcrafted just for me.

I'll have to move to a lake and eat soggy bread crumbs with ducks.

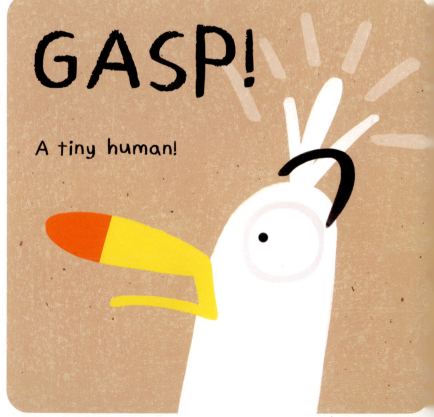

MUNCH

CRUNCHY
CRUNCH
CRUNCH

MUNCH
MUNCH

Back. Away. Slowly. They can be VERY unpredictable. If this thing comes any closer, get ready to—

Bye-bye, nice crabby.

Short Stuff, you're a genius!

Hi. Could we please have some?

Thanks.
Nice sandcastle.

If you don't want
the crust, we'll be
right here.

We like lying on our bellies, too.
And crackers.

You know, you got guts, Little Pal.
Is it all right if I call you Little Pal?

With your charm and my one-of-a-kind good looks, we make a great team. Maybe even the best! So just stick with me and you'll go places. No doubt about it.

Time to turn on that charm, Little Pal!
They're busting out the marshmallows!